Emily
SUMMER
OF GOLD

JULIE LAWSON

**Look for the other Emily stories
in Our Canadian Girl**

EMILY
SUMMER
OF GOLD

JULIE LAWSON

PENGUIN
CANADA

PENGUIN CANADA

Published by the Penguin Group

Penguin Group (Canada), 10 Alcorn Avenue, Toronto, Ontario, Canada M4V 3B2
(a division of Pearson Penguin Canada Inc.)

Penguin Group (USA) Inc., 375 Hudson Street, New York, New York 10014, U.S.A.
Penguin Books Ltd, 80 Strand, London WC2R 0RL, England
Penguin Ireland, 25 St Stephen's Green, Dublin 2, Ireland (a division of Penguin Books Ltd)
Penguin Group (Australia), 250 Camberwell Road, Camberwell, Victoria 3124, Australia
(a division of Pearson Australia Group Pty Ltd)
Penguin Books India Pvt Ltd, 11 Community Centre, Panchsheel Park, New Delhi – 110 017, India
Penguin Group (NZ), Cnr Airborne and Rosedale Roads, Albany, Auckland, New Zealand
(a division of Pearson New Zealand Ltd)
Penguin Books (South Africa) (Pty) Ltd, 24 Sturdee Avenue, Rosebank, Johannesburg 2196,
South Africa

Penguin Books Ltd, Registered Offices: 80 Strand, London WC2R 0RL, England

First published 2004

1 2 3 4 5 6 7 8 9 10   (WEB)

Copyright © Julie Lawson, 2004
Cover and interior illustrations © Janet Wilson, 2004
Design: Matthews Communications Design Inc.
Map © Sharon Matthews

Manufactured in Canada.

LIBRARY AND ARCHIVES CANADA CATALOGUING IN PUBLICATION

Lawson, Julie, 1947–
Emily : summer of gold / Julie Lawson.

(Our Canadian girl)
"Emily, book four".
ISBN 0-14-301672-5

I. Title. II. Title: Summer of gold. III. Series.

PS8573.A933E476 2004   jC813'.54   C2004-903059-0

Visit the Penguin Group (Canada) website at **www.penguin.ca**

For Charlayne

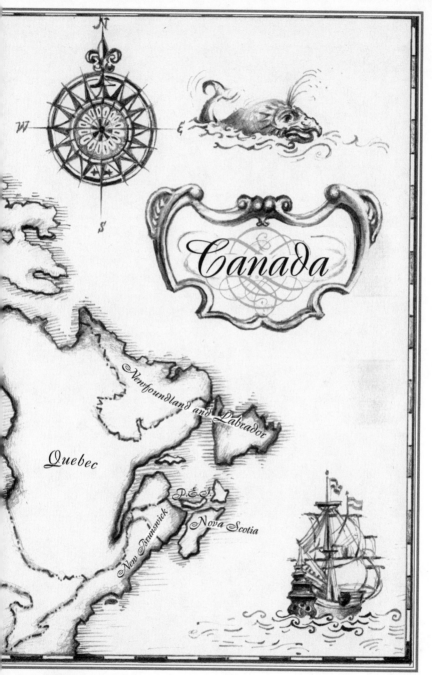

N

W — E

S

Canada

Newfoundland and Labrador

Quebec

P.E.I.

New Brunswick

Nova Scotia

 Marks the location of the story

THE LAST CHAPTER
OF EMILY'S TALE

I N AUGUST 1896, on a remote creek in the Klondike River Valley, Yukon, three men made a chance discovery that launched the biggest gold rush in history. Prospectors lucky enough to be in the region staked claims that would eventually produce nearly seven million dollars worth of gold.

At the time of the discovery, however, winter was already closing in on the north. It wasn't until July 1897, when two gold-laden steamers arrived in San Francisco and Seattle, that news of the bonanza reached the outside world. Within days, the Klondike Stampede was on.

The first stage of the journey was by steamboat—up the Pacific coast to Alaska and the start of the rigorous overland trails. Thousands of gold seekers swarmed into west coast ports, desperate to reach Dawson City, the heart of the goldfields, before winter set in.

Thousands more waited until the spring of 1898. Of the one hundred thousand people who set out, fewer than half actually made it. And among those, a very small number found gold.

The city of Victoria, situated on the tip of Vancouver Island, was a natural starting point. Before boarding a ship, however, those heading for the Klondike had to buy an "outfit"—enough food, clothing, and supplies to last a year. Americans learned that if they bought their outfits in Canada, they would not have to pay duty taxes when crossing the border from Alaska into Yukon Territory.

This was a golden opportunity for Victoria businesses, especially those who became "outfitters for the Klondike." And if anyone had a dog for sale—a dog strong enough to pull a heavily loaded sleigh—that person could name the price.

News of the gold discovery is not yet known when we open the final chapter of Emily's story. It is June 1897, a few days after the celebration of Queen Victoria's Diamond Jubilee. Emily is enjoying her summer holiday, but the days are a bit of a letdown after the excitement of the Jubilee. What could possibly match the thrilling spectacle of fireworks or the sight of Victoria's new parliament buildings lit up in honour of the Queen?

Emily is about to find out! When news of the Klondike Gold Rush reaches Victoria, residents are swept up in a fever of excitement that surpasses that of the Jubilee. Even Emily's father is affected.

What changes will the gold rush bring to Emily, her family, and her friends?

"Summer holidays!" Emily sang the words out loud. She'd left her house a few minutes earlier and was now biking along Dallas Road with the sea to her right, Beacon Hill to her left, the wind at her back, and a fine morning stretching ahead.

She swerved to avoid a pothole, narrowly missed another and, ringing her bicycle bell, flew past a horse-drawn carriage to escape the dust and dried manure kicked up by the horses' hooves. Beyond the carriage, the road was clear and the air held nothing but the scent of wild roses and the salty tang of the sea.

She kept to the road until she came to a grassy field overlooking the strait. Ignoring the bumps, she rode straight across the field to the edge of the cliff and dismounted. She left her bicycle in a thicket of rose bushes and clambered down the steep path to the beach.

Two months of holidays! After the excitement of Queen Victoria's Diamond Jubilee, Emily was afraid that the summer might be boring. She was also saddened by the possibility that she and her best friend, Alice, might not be able to see each other until they went back to school in September.

But today Emily was optimistic. She had other good friends, like Hing's daughter, Mei Yuk, and George Walsh. She had her sisters, Jane and Amelia, and her bicycle, and as of this morning, she had a plan—to go places where she might see Alice by chance. They both had bicycles, and they liked the same places. It was such a simple and obvious plan that she couldn't imagine why she hadn't thought of it sooner.

When she reached the bottom of the path, she surveyed the empty beach with high hopes. If Alice *were* to show up on a beach, this would be the one. They'd spent hours here in the past, hunting for treasures, building forts out of driftwood, splashing in the cold water, paddling on logs. George had often joined them, along with Alice's brother, Tom.

Emily grimaced at the thought of Tom. He'd always been a bit of a rascal, but not the bully he was now—picking on Mei Yuk and her brothers, sneering at Emily, making rude comments. Thank goodness *he* wasn't on the beach. Her morning would've been ruined if he had been.

She sat on a log and opened her sketchbook, pleased that she'd brought it along. She needed the practice. Besides, sketching on a beach was the very thing that Emily Carr, her art teacher, liked to do.

Pencil poised, she looked about for something to draw. Sandpipers running along the shore? The rocky outcrop? The steamship crossing the strait, with the mountains in the background? She'd sketched the mountains many times before, but why not? The ship would be a challenge. Recalling Miss Carr's words about shape and form, she began.

Several sketches later, and with still no sign of Alice, Emily closed her sketchbook and set off to do some beachcombing. She was strolling along, pausing now and then to pocket a smooth stone or a seashell, when she saw a mob of crows and sea-gulls swooping over something on the beach. From a distance, it looked like a bundle of dark clothing. But as she got closer, she saw that it was a dog.

A dead dog.

Her heart gave a turn. How long had the poor thing been lying there? His fur was still wet. Had the tide washed him in? Had he made it to shore on his own, only to give up at the end?

He'd been a fine-looking dog—medium in size, black with a white chest and muzzle, tan markings on his paws, a long tail, and pointed ears. But he was so thin! His ribs—

"Oh!" Emily started, wide-eyed with shock. The dog's chest was moving. His tail twitched. A tremor passed through his body. "You're alive!" Emily gasped. "It's a miracle!"

The dog made a horrible retching sound and struggled to his feet. Shaking uncontrollably, he heaved up buckets of seawater until finally, spent and exhausted, he collapsed again.

"Don't give up now!" Emily cried in alarm.

He whimpered at the sound of her voice and made a feeble attempt to wag his tail. Another tremor passed through him.

Emily leaned over and felt his side. In spite of the sunshine, he was freezing. And no wonder—the waters in the strait never warmed up, not even in the summer.

She took off her pinafore, wrapped it around the dog, and began to rub him down. "You must be a strong swimmer," she said. "As strong as Samson in the Bible story, only Samson wasn't a dog. I think that's what I'll call you. Samson, but Sam for short. Do you like that name?"

The dog gave another whimper, more like a sigh. He was still shivering.

"There, there, Sam," Emily murmured. "I'll take care of you."

First, she had to get him home. The nearest path to the top of the cliffs was only a few yards away. It was longer than the path she'd come down on, but since it wasn't as steep, she knew it would be an easier climb.

She picked Sam up and held him against her chest. He was as light as a rag doll but so cold that she too began to shiver.

But not for long! By the time she reached the road, she was drenched with sweat. With every step, Sam had grown heavier. Now he was start-ing to wheeze. "Easy, boy," she soothed. "We're almost there …"

Almost? Her house was still three long blocks away. She'd never make it. She'd have to stop somewhere and rest, or leave Sam and run home to get her mother.

Just then, she heard the Beacon Hill streetcar

clang to a stop behind her. As luck would have it, a familiar Scottish voice called out, "Hello, Emily! Need a hand?"

She turned and saw her neighbour stepping off the platform. "Mr. Sinclair! Am I glad to see you!"

He caught up to her and gently lifted Sam into his arms. "You're about done in, lass," he said. "You *and* the dog."

"Isn't he beautiful? I'm calling him Sam. I found him on the beach." She let Mr. Sinclair carry Sam until they reached her house, then insisted she could manage on her own. "I can't wait to show everyone," she said, and thanked him again.

Her sisters had spotted her from an upstairs window and came running outside, shrieking with delight.

"A dog! Emily's got a dog!"

"Where did you get him? Why's he shivering?"

"Mother, hurry! Emily's got a dog!"

"How come you're carrying him?"

"What's his name?"

"His name's Sam," Emily told them. "And you have to speak quietly. You're scaring him."

Mother met them on the back verandah. "Oh, Emily. Look at you. And this poor creature ..."

"I'm calling him Sam."

"Well, Sam needs some attention and you need dry clothes. Away you go—and mind you have a good wash."

Emily reluctantly left Sam in the kitchen and did as she was told. A short time later, she came back and found him lying by the wood stove, wrapped in warm blankets and sleeping soundly.

Jane and Amelia were watching over him. "He drank some water," Jane reported. "And a bit of beef broth."

"Mother told us to pat him, to move his blood," said Amelia.

Emily smiled. "Doesn't he look contented? At first, I thought he was dead. But then he came to life before my very eyes." She told them the story, then bent down and planted a kiss on Sam's white muzzle. "I love him already."

"I know, dear," said Mother. "But don't get your hopes up."

"What? I can keep him, can't I?"

"Not if he belongs to someone else. He may have been trying to get home, you know. In any case, we'll see what your father has to say."

CHAPTER № 2

The possibility that Sam could be someone else's dog hadn't occurred to Emily, and she quickly put the thought from her mind. She kept herself busy while waiting for her father by washing the lunch dishes, pulling carrots from the garden, and helping Jane shell some green peas. She watered the garden, too, using the outside pump to fill one watering can after another.

Every few minutes, she went inside to check on Sam. Was he awake or asleep? Was he warm enough? Did he have enough water? Had he drunk more broth?

By late afternoon, he was beginning to stir. Emily mashed up some leftover beef stew and fed him a small amount. "Good dog," she said. "This will fatten you up."

He wagged his tail and took a few shaky steps around the kitchen, exploring the various nooks and corners before returning to his spot by the stove.

Emily kneeled beside him, stroking his head. If she biked to the James Bay Bridge and met her father on his way home from work, they could walk back together and she could tell him all about Sam. So by the time—

All at once she remembered. "My bicycle! I left it on the cliff!"

"Quick, then!" Mother said. "Go back and get it."

Emily rushed off in a flap. How careless! She was everything a girl who wanted a dog should *not* be—forgetful, absent-minded, scatterbrained— what would Father say now? She couldn't have ridden her bicycle with Sam, but she should have gone right back to get it. And her sketch-book! She'd forgotten that, too.

At least she remembered where she'd left her bicycle. She headed straight for the rose thicket—but the bicycle was gone. She searched all around the cliff, the path, and finally, the beach. Her sketchbook was still on the log. But there was no sign of her bicycle.

She choked back a sob. Who would take a girl's bicycle? Especially one with faded ribbons tied to the spokes?

She trudged home tearfully, dreading the moment she would have to face her father.

He was home when she arrived. He listened to her story and agreed that she'd been careless but understandably so, given her concern about the dog. He also pointed out that the bicycle may well have gone missing while she was still on the beach.

He wrote out a description, asked Emily for more details about where and when she'd last seen the bicycle, and left for town. He was going straight to the police station to file a report.

He returned a short time later and announced that he'd also stopped by the newspaper office and placed an ad about the dog. "If no one claims him by the end of the week," he said, "Sam can stay. But don't count your bridges."

"Chickens!" Amelia corrected. "Don't count your chickens before they're hatched."

"Quite so. As long as you all understand and don't get too attached to the dog."

"I already am," said Emily.

Her father wagged a finger in her direction. "As long as you realize that someone might be missing Sam as much as you are missing your bicycle. Meanwhile, I'm going to ask Dr. Murphy to drop by and have a look."

"He's a horse doctor!" Jane blurted.

"A veterinarian treats all animals, Jane. He'll be able—"

"Worms, too?" Amelia wondered. "And slugs?"

"They're not animals," said Jane.

"Are too."

"Are not!"

"Are too! And cows."

"Girls!" Father silenced them with a look. "Dr. Murphy will decide if Sam's basically healthy or if he needs any special treatment. Now, after walking back and forth to town three times within the last hour, I'm ready for my dinner."

Emily waited anxiously for the week to pass, fearing that a stranger might show up at any moment to take back the dog. Happily, no one came. At the end of the week, Sam was welcomed as an official member of the Murdoch family.

Dr. Murphy had told them that Sam was about two years old and most likely a mix of border collie and Labrador, with a fair bit of something else. He couldn't say how the dog had ended up in the water. Sam's previous owner might have gone off in a boat and left him behind. Maybe the dog had tried to follow. Maybe there'd been a boating accident. Or maybe the owner had purposely dumped Sam overboard to be rid of him. Sadly, people did take such actions. The fact that Sam had survived, in spite of his under-nourished condition, showed great strength, endurance, and determination.

Before leaving, Dr. Murphy had praised Emily for being such a fine judge of canine character.

"She was born in the Year of the Dog," Jane had remarked, as if that explained everything.

Over the next few weeks, Sam's health slowly improved. His nose stayed cold and moist, his coat began to shine, and his eyes became bright and alert. On daily walks to Beacon Hill Park, Emily and her sisters taught him to sit, stay, and heel. Later, they taught him to fetch, to shake a paw, and to say *please*.

Emily refused to let Jane teach him to play dead, not after he'd had such a near-death experi-ence. And as for dressing him up, she was furious when she discovered Sam wearing Amelia's Sunday bonnet and an apron. "How could you, Amelia?" she fumed. "He's not a doll! See how he's hanging his head? He's embarrassed!"

"He likes it," Amelia pouted.

"Well, it's not dignified for a canine. So don't do it again."

"Bossy," Amelia muttered and stuck out her tongue.

Sam learned quickly. Emily liked to think it was all her doing, but Sam may well have been taught the basics by someone in his former home. And she had to give her family some credit. It took a few harsh words from Mother and Father before Sam stopped rolling in the flower beds and burying bones in the vegetable garden.

"How could you, Amelia?"
Emily fumed. "He's not a doll!"

"What a handsome dog! So well behaved and obedient!"

Emily smiled at the passersby as she led Sam through the busy section of town. Although she wasn't solely responsible for his behaviour, she basked in the praise.

She was on her way to Chinatown for her weekly visit with Mei Yuk and, for the first time, she was taking Sam. She'd tied a leash to his collar to make sure he didn't run off, and he was behaving admirably. It was a wonder, with so many distractions. People, horses, dogs, carriages, wagons, streetcars, a herd of cattle being driven down to the wharf—the noise and traffic were enough to distract anyone.

And the smells! Sam tried to stop at the butcher's shop, where sides of beef and strings of pork sausage hung temptingly over the board-walk, but Emily was firm. "Come, Sam," she said. "We'll stop for a bone on the way back."

She, too, was finding it hard not to be distracted. She hadn't walked to Chinatown in a long time, and it seemed much farther than when she'd taken her bicycle. She'd been so happy with Sam she hadn't really missed her bicycle, not *terribly,* but now she looked at bicycles in the street, hoping she might spot her own. What could have happened to it? Would she ever get it back? Sam would love running alongside as she biked to the park or to the waterfront or through town.

At last, they reached Chinatown. Emily turned down a brick alley, crossed a narrow lane, and found herself in the courtyard behind Hing's restaurant. "Mei Yuk!" she called, seeing her friend through the kitchen window. "Come and meet Sam."

Mei Yuk gave a cheerful wave and hurried outside, followed by her father.

"You can pet him if you like," said Emily. "He's very friendly."

Mei Yuk crouched down and reached out her hand. Sam gave it a sniff and, smelling something tasty, began to lick her fingers.

Hing laughed. "He like Hing special chicken, same as Em-ry."

"We taught him some tricks," Emily said. "Watch." She put Sam through his paces, ending with, "Sam, lie down."

He yawned, circled three times, and obeyed.

"May I leave him out here while we have our English lesson?" Emily asked.

"No, we do the lesson here," Mei Yuk said. "Please, Father? Too hot inside."

Hing agreed, and with his help they pulled together some crates and boards to make a couple of desks.

While Mei Yuk was upstairs gathering her books, Emily went into the kitchen to say hello to Mei Yuk's mother and brothers. She came out a short time later with a bowl of water and a big juicy bone. "Say *please,*" she said.

At that moment, Mei Yuk appeared. "Remember, Em-ry?" she laughed. "First lesson. Mei Yuk, sit. Mei Yuk, stand. Now, Sam, sit. Sam, stand. Sam, say *please!*"

Emily joined in the laughter, remembering how difficult their first lesson had been and how much Mei Yuk had learned since then. She could draw, too, even without taking art lessons.

That gave Emily an idea. She opened her satchel and took out her sketchbook. "Mei Yuk, would you draw me a picture of Sam? I tried, but you're much better."

"Thank you," Mei Yuk said modestly. She observed Sam stretched out on the cobblestones, gnawing on his bone. With a few bold strokes and a little shading, she managed to capture what Emily called "the essence of his canine character."

To finish, Mei Yuk took a red pencil from her box and printed *Emily Dog Sam* at the top of the page. "Red is for good luck," she said.

Emily hugged her friend. She felt that she ought to mention the apostrophe *s* that Mei Yuk had left out, but since it was summer and she wasn't a real teacher anyway, she let it go.

The lesson passed quickly with a bit of reading, some printing, and an easy spelling test.

As Emily was getting ready to leave, Hing came out to say goodbye. "Be careful," he said. "Watch Sam. Many people want dog today."

"Why?" Emily was puzzled.

"For new Gold Mountain." Before he could go on, a startled cry came from the kitchen, followed by a clatter of pots and a hiss of steam. "Aie, Bak Cheun!" He rushed inside, uttering a string of words that Emily didn't understand.

"Bak Cheun learn to cook," Mei Yuk said sympathetically. "He make … mistake?"

"Mistakes," Emily corrected. "More than one."

Mei Yuk nodded. "Many mistakes. Like me, in spelling."

"No, Mei Yuk! You almost had a perfect score today. Next week, you'll do even better."

With that, Emily left for home.

By now it was late afternoon, and the streets were busier than ever. People were gathering on the boardwalks and in shop doorways, talking with an unusual amount of fervour.

"Have you heard …?"

"… leaving first thing tomorrow."

"Terrible shame to miss it … you know what they say about the early bird …"

"… a bonanza!"

Block after block, Emily heard snippets of similar conversations. Something was afoot. There was a feeling of celebration, as if it were Christmas, the Diamond Jubilee, and the 24th of May all rolled into one. Why, on an ordinary Tuesday?

She had just passed the butcher's shop when she spotted Mr. Sinclair across the street. He was talking to a group of men, his face flushed with excitement. *He'd* tell her what was going on.

She stopped on the edge of the boardwalk, waited for a streetcar to pass, and stepped onto the street. "Come, Sam. Heel!" She tugged on his leash, but it came loose in her hand and Sam bounded away. "Sam!" she yelled anxiously. He couldn't go far, but with so many people around, anything might happen.

She turned to follow Sam and spotted him at once. The rascal! He was sitting outside the butcher's shop, unabashedly wagging his tail as a bearded stranger fed him sausages.

"Sam, come here!" Emily commanded.

He gave her a guilty look, gulped down another sausage, and slunk towards her, tail between his legs.

"Bad dog!" she said, retying the leash to his collar. "You know you're to come when you're called."

"Nice dog you got there," the sausage man remarked. "Can he pull a sled?"

The question took Emily by surprise. "Probably! But only in the winter."

"Too bad," he said. "I can't wait that long."

Emily frowned but didn't stop to ask what he meant. Why would he care if Sam could pull a sled? And what was the big hurry? His comments were as strange as Hing's remark about Gold Mountain. What was *that* supposed to mean? She knew that the Chinese had once used the expression to describe British Columbia as a land of golden opportunities. Hing had been one of thousands who'd come to work on the railway many years ago, but whose dreams of wealth had not come true. Did a new Gold Mountain mean another railway was being built? If so, why would people want a dog?

At dinner that evening, Emily talked about her day and asked her father if he'd noticed anything unusual in town.

"I did, as a matter of fact," he said. "And I'll tell you why. Some people came up from Seattle this afternoon with word of a gold discovery. What Hing probably meant by 'Gold Mountain' was that a lot of people will put their dreams into something that won't come true. You know how it is. Word spreads and the story gets bigger and people get carried away."

"Like making a mole out of a molehill," said Amelia.

"No, silly," Jane laughed. "It's a *mountain* out of a molehill."

"Quite so," said Father. "It could be nothing at all."

He couldn't have been more wrong.

CHAPTER N° 4

Seattle Is Wild! Rush for the Gold!

The newspaper headlines made it official. By the following day, Victoria was as wild as Seattle. The ripple of excitement that Emily had noticed had swollen into a frenzy. Newsboys, clerks, shopkeepers, hack drivers, streetcar conductors, friends, neighbours—everyone had something to say. After all, it was no ordinary discovery. It was a bonanza—an exceptionally large and rich discovery of gold.

"I'll never get my shopping done," Emily's mother complained. She and the girls had taken the streetcar to town, but every time they turned around, they were stopped by someone wanting to spread the news.

Mr. Saunders, the butcher, was the latest to hold them up. "Have you heard?" he asked. "Three prospectors up in the Yukon were panning for gold on a little creek and now they're million-aires. Arrived in Seattle two days ago with their baggage so full of nuggets they could hardly lug it off the ship."

And so it went, in one shop after another.

"... picking up nuggets by the handful!"

"Nuggets the size of potatoes ..."

"When's the next ship heading north? Where can I buy a ticket?"

"Emily!" George waved from a newsstand across the street and ran over to join her. "Have you heard the news? I read in the paper that a prospector found a slab of gold as thick as a slice of cheddar cheese!"

Amelia giggled. "You could have a gold sandwich!"

"And break your teeth, silly Millie."

"Jane Pain." Amelia shot back. "Georgie Porgie ..."

George ignored her. "Can you imagine? What an adventure! I wish I were old enough to go."

"Me, too!" squealed Amelia.

"We *all* wish you could go," said Jane.

At that moment, Mrs. Murdoch came out of the druggist's. "At last I'm done!" She exchanged a few words with George and ushered the girls off to their streetcar stop.

On the way, Emily saw Tom and his father standing with a group of men outside the tobacconist's. She cringed, expecting Tom to give her a nasty look as she walked by, or to mutter something. But he was listening so intently to one of the men that he didn't even notice her.

"Soon as I'm packed, I'm off to the Klondike," Emily overhead the man say. "But listen, fellas, you've got to act fast if you want some of that gold ..." The rest of his words were lost in the hubbub of the street.

Gold, gold, and more gold. Emily couldn't believe it. Was she living in the same Victoria? You'd think the gold had been found in Beacon Hill Park, not in some faraway place called the Klondike.

Where exactly was the Klondike? Was it true what she'd overheard, that the sun shone at midnight in the summer, but in winter there was no sunlight at all?

When they reached the car stop, Emily asked her mother if she'd heard anything new in the druggist's.

"Well, yes," Mother said. "Mr. Sinclair wants to sell his store so that he can go to the Klondike. So far, it's only a rumour."

By now, more people were gathering at the stop. Emily listened in on their conversations and tried to sort out the facts from the growing number of rumours.

"... going up north on a bicycle!"

"Mr. Shotbolt, the druggist? He put up a sign saying that Vaseline's a cure for frostbite, and he sold every last jar in minutes."

"Gold fever? It's an epidemic! You bet there's a cure, but it can only be found in the Yukon …"

By the time they got home, Emily was so muddled with the news that she no longer knew what to think.

"Is the gold rush a true story?" Amelia wondered. "Or is it a fairy tale?"

Jane rolled her eyes. "Of course it's true. People read it in the newspaper and newspapers don't lie."

"Father always brings home a newspaper," Emily reminded them. "When he gets home, we can read about it for ourselves."

Surprisingly, Father did not come home with a newspaper that evening, and at dinner he was unusually quiet. Not quiet, worried, but quiet, excited. As if he were holding a secret he couldn't wait to tell.

While everyone else was talking about the news they'd heard in town or listening to Amelia's story about dressing a friend's cat in doll clothes—since "bossy Emily" wouldn't let her play dress-up with Sam—Emily observed her father. His eyes twinkled. His face glowed. He gazed at Mother with a curious half-smile on his face. And when he caught Emily's eye, he actually winked.

Emily was so taken aback by this uncharacteristic gesture she almost choked on her pudding. Whatever the secret was, it must be something wonderful.

Suddenly, her heart dropped into her stomach. What if Father was thinking of going to the Klondike?

No! She almost laughed out loud. He was a banker, not someone who went off on adventures.

Still, his behaviour was odd. He kept glancing at his watch. Was he expecting someone?

Was a special parcel about to be delivered? Not this late in the day. And there was nothing the girls had to be on time for, except bed, and that was hardly—oh! Perhaps he was waiting to tell Mother something in private. Maybe he was planning to give her a special gift. That had to be it.

The next time he looked at Emily, she gave him a knowing smile and winked—and winked again, to be sure he understood.

She was enjoying the novelty of sharing a secret with her father until Amelia said, "Emily's got something in her eye. She keeps making faces and blinking funny."

"I do not!" Emily glared. Trust Amelia to spoil things.

That night, as soon as she knew that Amelia was asleep, Emily nudged Jane and whispered, "Do you want to hear a secret?"

"Yes!" Jane was instantly awake.

Emily cautioned her to be quiet and told her what she'd observed during dinner. "So now I'm going to sneak downstairs and listen."

"It's not polite to eavesdrop," said Jane. "So if we get caught it was your idea."

Emily agreed. They got out of bed and tiptoed downstairs to the parlour door.

"Eldorado at last!" Father was saying. "Fortune's smiling on us, my dear. A once-in-a-lifetime opportunity."

"You can't be serious!" said Mother.

"Think of it. Here we are, in the right place at the right time, and with a fair bit of grit and perseverance, we'll have a comfortable income. Walsh feels the same way."

"Oh, John! Please …"

"Let me tell you all about it."

Emily looked at Jane, her heart pounding with

apprehension and dread. If what she was thinking were true, no wonder Father wanted Mother to be the first to know.

They crept upstairs and slipped into bed. "Eldorado has to do with gold, doesn't it?" Jane said quietly. "But what's grit? What did Father mean?"

"Grit means determination. You know what I think?" Emily whispered in Jane's ear.

"But it's so far!" Jane started to cry.

"Be quiet!" Amelia raised her head, took one look at her sister, and said, "Jane, what's wrong?"

"Father's got gold fever!" she sobbed.

Amelia frowned. "He didn't look sick," she said sleepily.

"Not that kind of fever." Emily struggled to hold back her tears. "He's planning to go to the Klondike!"

CHAPTER N° 5

Emily braced herself. She had joined her parents for breakfast and now looked from one to the other, knowing that the moment had come.

She'd spent half the night fretting about her father, but then another thought had loomed in her mind. What if he were planning to take the whole family to the Klondike? She didn't mind a bit of snow in the winter, but no sunlight? No beaches, no Beacon Hill, no art classes with Miss Carr? She'd hate it! How could she leave Mei Yuk? And what about Alice? They could never be friends if Emily were a million miles away.

After worrying herself into a restless sleep, she'd woken up early and gone downstairs, determined to find out what her father meant to do.

She forced down a mouthful of porridge, swallowed some milk, and boldly said, "I was eavesdropping last night. I'm sorry. I know it was wrong, but ... oh, Father! Please don't go to the Klondike. I'm sure it's a good opportunity and you have lots of grit, but it's too far! And please don't make us go! Who would take care of the garden or do your work at the bank? If you don't want to go alone ..." Her breath caught in a sob. "I'll let you take Sam. But you mustn't stay away too long because he'll forget his training and I'll miss him so terribly ..."

Her voice trailed off as she noticed the amused expressions on her parents' faces. "It's not funny," she said, hurt that they hadn't taken her seriously.

Father leaned over and kissed her cheek. "Dear Emily. Of course it isn't funny. And thank you for offering Sam. It was a kind and thoughtful gesture. But you ought not to eavesdrop, and this is a case in point. You misunderstood what you heard. I'm not going anywhere, certainly not to the Klondike."

Surprised, Emily turned to her mother. "But you sounded so upset."

"I was cautious, dear, and only at first. Once I heard your father's plan, I became rather excited."

"And here's the plan." Father smiled. "Mr. Walsh and I are going to buy Mr. Sinclair's store."

"What?" Emily gaped. "It's true? Mr. Sinclair is selling his store? But he sells hats and clothes, not money. You and Mr. Walsh are bankers."

"Not any more. We're leaving the bank and running our own business. Because even though we're not going north, there are thousands who are, and come next spring there'll be thousands more. And what will they need? Not just hats and clothing, but all sorts of tools and supplies. Everything from candles to gold pans. And where do you think they'll buy them?" He winked.

"From your store?"

"That's right! From Murdoch and Walsh— Outfitters for the Klondike."

The new outfitters had to act quickly, for competition was fierce. Gold-seekers were arriving in droves, from all over the continent, and stores that sold *anything* related to a Klondike expedition were doing a booming business. In a short time, Murdoch and Walsh had increased Mr. Sinclair's stock, bought all manner of food and supplies from the Victoria warehouses, and erected a new sign. Then they placed an announcement in the newspaper saying that they were ready to open.

On the day of the grand opening, Emily accompanied her father to the store. They walked through town, marvelling at how Victoria had transformed since the news of the gold rush. Men dressed in the typical Klondike clothing of canvas coats, knee-high boots, and wide-brimmed hats were now a familiar sight, and the festive atmosphere showed no signs of fading.

Emily had never known her father to be so excited. He had indeed caught gold fever—the stay-at-home kind, thank goodness—and she couldn't help but catch it as well. Especially since she'd been given a special job at the opening.

Murdoch and Walsh—Klondike Outfitters! The store looked very grand with its eye-catching sign stretched across the front. The display windows were filled with items a gold miner would need, from arctic socks, moosehide parkas, and heavy woollen underwear to prospectors' picks and shovels. "Klondike sleighs" hung in rows against the outside wall, and portable "Yukon stoves," especially designed in Victoria, had been placed on the boardwalk.

Emily had been astounded the first time she'd seen a similar display. Sleighs, in Victoria, in summer? Now, such displays were commonplace.

It wasn't long before the first customers began to arrive. Emily's job—better than any chore she could imagine—was to stand at the doorway and offer everyone a candy. George stood beside her. When he wasn't trying to pinch a sweet, he was handing out complete lists of what a Klondike traveller would need.

By mid-morning, Emily was almost out of candy. A steady stream of customers had been entering the store. Many were from the United States. They were buying their outfits in Canada so they wouldn't have to pay duty taxes when they entered the Canadian Yukon. Other customers had purchased their outfits elsewhere but had forgotten a few essential items.

One fellow came out of the store in such high spirits that he gave Emily a handful of his candies instead of taking one of hers. "I can't believe my luck!" he said. Beaming, he held up a copy of *The Complete Works of William Shakespeare*. "A book is hard to come by in the north, and without one to keep me company over the winter, I'd go stark-raving mad."

Another fellow came out with a sleigh

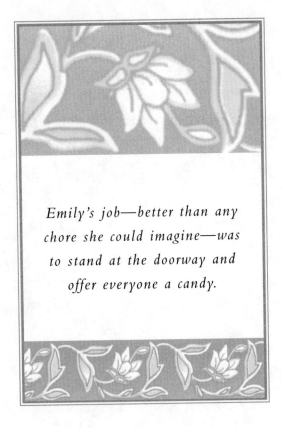

Emily's job—better than any chore she could imagine—was to stand at the doorway and offer everyone a candy.

strapped to his back and a hefty bundle of goods. "They've got everything I need in there except for a dog," he said. "Either of you kids know where I can get a good one? One that could pull a sled? I'll pay up to four hundred dollars."

"Emily's got a dandy," George said. "But he's not for sale."

"Then you better keep an eye on him, Miss. There are a lot of desperate men about." So saying, he shifted his load and ambled off.

Emily gave George a worried look. "Nobody would steal Sam … would they?"

"They might try."

His words were not encouraging. Emily had left Sam at home and wouldn't be back before noon. What if Jane or Amelia took him for a walk and the leash came off, like before? What if someone else tempted him with sausages and tried to lure him away? As soon as the bonbons were gone, she'd go home to make sure everything was all right. And she'd have to train Sam to resist temptation.

"Good morning, Em-ry!"

It was Mei Yuk and Hing. "Welcome to Murdoch and Walsh," Emily said proudly. "Here, have a bonbon."

"Thank you," said Mei Yuk. "Like Chinese New Year, when merchant give special food."

"And read this." George handed Hing a list of supplies. "Everything you need to make the journey in comfort."

"Hing's not going—" Emily's smile vanished when she saw how closely Hing was studying the list. "You're not going to the Klondike, are you?"

"No, I am too old and too smart for new Gold Mountain. But list is good, for practise English."

"Ha! Good luck."

Emily recognized the voice and its snarky tone, and knew right away it was Tom. She moved protectively towards Mei Yuk as Tom approached, his father close behind.

"Come," Hing said to Mei Yuk. "We look in store."

"So *rong*," Tom said with a smirk. Then, to Emily, "Got a candy for me? One without any germs?"

Before she could answer, he'd scooped up a handful of bonbons and stuffed them into his pocket.

"Tom!" Mr. Kerr gestured from the doorway. "You coming or not?"

"Yes, sir," Tom said and followed his father into the store.

Emily looked around for Alice, hoping she might have come along, but there was no sign of her or her mother.

Customers continued to arrive throughout the morning, and no one left the store empty-handed. Even friends and neighbours who had dropped by to encourage the new owners found something to buy.

Emily couldn't hide her astonishment when Mr. Sinclair, the former owner, entered the store. A short time later, he came out brandishing a receipt. "Murdoch and Walsh have thought of everything," he announced to a group of men examining the Yukon stoves. "Order an outfit and they'll deliver it straight to the wharf, sealed up and labelled to a T."

"Mr. Sinclair!" Emily burst out. "Are *you* going to the Klondike?"

"Don't sound so alarmed!" he chuckled. "I'm not all that long in the tooth."

Emily blushed. "I'm sorry, I didn't mean it like that. It's just that you're the only person I *know* who's going. When do you leave? Is Mrs. Sinclair going, too?"

"Nope, the missus is staying behind. And I'm off on the *Bristol* in four weeks' time. So if you want to sell Sam, let me know."

"I'd never sell Sam!"

"I know, lass. I'm only teasing."

His comment prompted an even greater urgency to make sure that Sam was safe. Since it was now close to noon and Emily's basket of bonbons was almost empty, she said goodbye to George and her father and hurried home.

She needn't have worried. The moment she turned down her street she saw Sam. He was lying beneath the maple tree, right where she'd told him to stay. "Here, Sam!" she called.

His ears pricked up. With a hearty woof, he bounded over to greet her with such exuberance, you'd think she'd been gone for months.

"I missed you, too!" She hugged him as he slapped wet kisses all over her face, his tail wagging so vigorously it almost knocked her over.

Jane and Amelia were watching from the front verandah. "He wouldn't even come for a walk," Jane said. "Just lay there whining, *Emily, Emily,* all morning long."

"Not *all* morning," Amelia corrected. "We put on his leash and *tried* to take him for a walk, but he wouldn't budge."

"He was as stubborn as a mule," Jane added. "He dug in his feet so hard it was worse than pulling up carrots in the garden."

"I'm glad," said Emily. She told her sisters how worried she'd been and why. "So we have to watch him all the time and not let anyone pet him or give him treats. Except for us."

CHAPTER N.º 6

"What now?" Emily muttered crossly. She was hot, sticky, and up to her elbows in raspberries, and Sam was barking down the house. One interruption after another! First the milkman had come. Then Mrs. Sinclair, with a basket of plums. Then the vegetable peddler. Now someone else was knocking on the back door.

"Hush, Sam! I'm coming!"

She'd been pleased at first. To be left on her own with the important task of making jam had made her feel grown-up and responsible. But now she was tired of cooking and stirring and straining, and she wished her mother would hurry up and get home.

She rinsed her hands, shook them dry, and wiped her hair from her sweaty forehead. "I'm coming, Sam! Be quiet!"

The last person she expected to see on opening the door was Alice.

They hadn't seen each other for weeks, and for a moment they just stood there, feeling somewhat shy. Then both started talking at once.

"I would've come—"

"It's been so long—"

They started to laugh. "You first," Emily said.

"I would've come sooner," said Alice, "but I wanted to clean it up first." She turned and looked over the railing.

Emily followed her gaze and gasped. Leaning against the verandah was her bicycle, as shiny as a new coin. The brass bell gleamed, and bright red and blue ribbons had replaced the tattered ones.

"Alice!" she cried. "I can't believe you found it. You, of all people!" She skipped down the stairs and hopped on for a ride around the yard. Sam ran at her side, yapping excitedly.

At the end of the ride, she rang the bell and gave the bicycle a fond pat. "When did you find it?" she asked, joining Alice on the steps. "And where? On the beach? In the park?"

Alice flushed with embarrassment. "I'm sorry to tell you this, but I found it the night before last … in our woodshed. Tom had hidden it in a corner. He said he took it for a joke. He was going to give it right back."

"He should've!" Emily fumed. "And he should've had the courage to bring it back himself. He ought to be punished. When Father tells the police—"

"I told Pa," Alice broke in quietly. "He nearly killed Tom." She looked as if she were about to say more, but she leaned forward instead and scratched Sam behind his ear. "Mei Yuk told me you had a dog."

Emily's mouth fell open. "You were talking to Mei Yuk?"

"Alice!" Emily cried.
*"I can't believe you found
it. You, of all people!"*

Alice nodded. "I saw her and Hing at your father's grand opening."

"When were you there? I looked for you after I saw Tom but didn't see you."

"You'd already gone home. Ma had to stop at the druggist's, so I waited for her while Tom and Pa went on ahead."

"And you talked to Mei Yuk?" Emily was astonished. "With your parents right there? And they didn't get after you?"

"They've had a lot of things on their mind lately," Alice said. "I doubt if they even noticed …" Her voice trailed off and she peered at Emily closely. "Have you cut your head? Your hair's covered with red streaks. And your face—"

"Oh, no! The jam!" Emily bolted inside and snatched the pot off the stove. The mixture had already begun to boil over. "Look at this mess!" she wailed. "Berry stains everywhere, the floor sticks like molasses—I'm doomed! When Mother comes home—"

"Fetch the mop and a bucket," Alice said

calmly. "I've been helping Ma with jams and jellies all week and believe me, I've had lots of practice cleaning up."

Together they set to work. By the time Emily's mother came home, the floor was mopped, the counter tops scrubbed, and the pot scoured, and six jars of raspberry jam were cooling on the counter. The only thing that wasn't gleaming was Emily.

"You've got measles!" Amelia shrieked when she saw her sister's face.

"I know," Emily said happily. "My pinafore's ruined and my hair's too sticky to brush and I don't give a hoot." In one afternoon, she'd regained her bicycle and seen Alice. It was one of the best days of her life.

CHAPTER 7

"Stop whining, Amelia!" Emily was rapidly losing her temper. That very morning in Sunday school she'd vowed to be more patient, but she hadn't counted on Amelia.

Why is it always Jane's turn? Stop being so bossy! Why can't we do what I want to do?

It didn't help when Jane kept reminding Amelia that since she was starting school in September, she'd better learn to behave.

The afternoon had started well. The Murdochs had taken the streetcar to the newly built Point Ellice Bridge, then walked along the Gorge waterway to the Walsh's house. While the grown-ups were inside celebrating the success of the new store, George had been entertaining the girls in the garden.

They'd spent the first hour playing croquet. Now George was letting them try out his bow and arrow.

"The target's too far away!" Amelia complained.

"We've already moved it once," said Jane.

"Well it's *still* too far!" She threw down the arrow and scowled.

"Then don't play!" The others carried on with their target shooting, determined to ignore her outbursts.

Finally, George, who'd been a model of patience, had had enough. "Look, Amelia," he said. "If you promise to stop whining, we'll do whatever you want to do."

She stuck out her lower lip. "But you don't have any dolls to play with. And no cats or dogs to dress up."

"So think of something else!" Jane said irritably. "Don't be such a baby."

"I'm not!" She furrowed her brow, trying to think of a grown-up game that didn't involve croquet mallets or arrows. "Can it be a 'let's pretend' game, like charades?"

"Yes!" Emily said. "I love charades!"

Amelia was quick to squash that idea. "I said a game *like* charades, and George said I could pick. So let's play ..." She scrunched up her face and thought for a moment. "Let's play gold rush!"

George raised his eyebrows in a question. "All right, but you'll have to tell us how to play."

"Well ... we pretend we're miners. We carry all the pretend supplies we bought from Murdoch and Walsh, and we take George's rowboat to the pretend Klondike."

"We could say it's on Deadman's Island," Emily suggested.

"And we pan for pretend gold!" added Jane.

They all warmed to the idea. Before long, they'd loaded the boat with a shovel and pick for digging, a skillet to use as a gold pan, and two travelling bags stuffed with rocks to serve as their supplies.

George was an enthusiastic rower, and since the island was only a half a mile down the Gorge, they were soon scrambling out of the boat and onto the shore.

Amelia waited until their gear was unloaded and the boat securely fastened, then gave further instructions. "We have to hike along the pretend trail, and everybody has to carry something. George can lead the way because he's a boy."

"Klondike, ho!" he shouted, and off they went.

Up and over the rocks, through a few dense thickets, in and out of the trees—they crossed the small island several times, grumbling about heavy loads, sore muscles, and aching backs, and moaning, "When are we going to get there?"

After the tenth time around, when their groaning was no longer pretend, Emily made a decision. "At last, we've made it!"

"Three cheers for the Klondike!" Jane said. "Hip, hip, hurray!"

"I say we start panning for gold!" said George.

"Me first! It was my idea." Amelia grabbed the skillet from Jane and began filling it with stones.

"Not like that," said Jane. "You scoop up gravel and water and swish it around."

"How do you know?"

"Because I saw a real miner in town showing everyone."

"I'm a miner—"

"A *whiner*."

"I am not!"

"Stop it!" Emily snapped. "Let George have a turn. He won't waste time squabbling. I'm going to dig for my gold."

She took the shovel and marched into the woods. *Sisters!* They were driving her to distraction. Amelia was getting impossible, and Jane made matters worse by egging her on. She wished someone would pack the pair of them off to the Klondike.

And that Tom, stealing her bicycle! He could go to the Klondike, too.

"Ooof!" She jabbed the shovel into a likely spot of earth. The ground was harder than it looked, but with a fair bit of muscle, some grit, and determination …

It wasn't long before she was panting with exertion. Her face was beaded with sweat and her dress stuck to her back and under her arms. Still, she had a sizable hole to show for her efforts, and the pile of dirt kept growing.

"Horrid, beastly Tom!" She punched out the words with every stab of the shovel. She was swinging back and forth, both feet on the blade, when she heard a burst of muffled laughter. George!

She whirled around and caught him leaning against a tree, shaking with mirth.

"How long have you been spying on me?" She was mortified that he might have heard her venting her anger.

"The whole time!" he hooted. "Why are you doing this? It's only pretend! You're not going to find any gold."

"I know that! I just felt like it." Better to stab at the ground than at her sisters. And stabbing at a pretend Tom didn't feel half bad.

She was about to carry on when she heard a loud splash followed by a chilling scream. "That sounds like Amelia!" Sick with fear, she threw down the shovel and started to run. "I never should have left them!" she cried as the screaming and splashing continued.

When she reached the shore and saw her sisters standing in the water, happily shrieking and splashing each other, her panic turned to anger. "What are you doing?" she yelled.

"Playing gold rush!" Laughing, the girls waded to shore. "Look inside the bags, Em. We found tons of gold. Fools' gold!"

"Yes," Amelia grinned, "and I fell into the creek and pretended I was drowning. Jane rescued me!"

"And then we got hot so we took a little dip."

"A *little* dip? Mother will be furious! Your hair, your clothes—You're drenched! And drowning isn't a game. How *could* you? Don't you remember—" She stopped abruptly, afraid that her anger would give way to tears.

It hadn't been so long ago that the Gorge waterway had echoed with screams. The old Point Ellice Bridge had collapsed, taking a fully loaded streetcar with it. Emily had been one of the passengers, and her memory of the disaster was still vivid, as was the terrifying sensation of being trapped underwater.

"I'll go back for the shovel," said George. "I think it's time we left."

Emily scowled at her sisters. "Now get in the rowboat and be quiet."

The girls protested but did as they were told. "You don't have be so bossy," Jane said. "You're not our mother."

"She's just pretending," said Amelia. "Aren't you, Em?"

"No! And if you think I'm bossy, wait till Mother and Father see you. And they'll blame me, since I'm the oldest."

There was a glum silence as they pushed off the boat and rowed away from the island. After a while, Jane said, "I'm sorry, Em. About the drowning. I wasn't thinking."

"Me, too," Amelia blubbered.

Emily gave them a stern look. "Well, now that you're both sorry, you'd better think of what you're going to tell Mother and Father."

"I'd better do some thinking myself," said George. "Just look at those travelling bags." Having been filled with rocks and gravel, and dragged around the island, the bags were wet and torn and filthy, both inside and out. "They looked fairly new when I took them out of the closet," he added.

The girls exchanged nervous glances. George's sombre tone and the state of the travelling bags made the whole situation worse.

As soon as the girls got home, they were sent to their room. They looked a disgrace after digging and kneeling in the dirt and tramping through the prickly underbrush. Their dresses and stockings were ripped and stained, Jane and Amelia were soaked, and Amelia could have drowned. Emily should have known better. There was no playing with Sam, no supper, and no sweets for a week. There were extra chores and letters of apology written to both sets of parents. All in all, they'd spoiled a splendid afternoon.

George, too, was being punished. Taking his mother's new travelling bags topped the list of his offences. Next came the skillet, scratched beyond any amount of scouring. And since he and Emily were the oldest, they were required to spend two afternoons a week until school started working in the storeroom of Murdoch and Walsh. Whatever wages they might have earned would be used to replace Mrs. Walsh's bags.

Emily paused from writing her apologies and listened to Sam whimpering at the back door. Poor thing. He was missing his playmates after being left alone, inside the house, for most of the day.

Amelia was whimpering, too. "How can I write a pology? I don't know how!"

"That's why you're going to school," Jane said. "So you'll learn. And it's an a-pology, not a *pology*."

"Stop correcting me! You're not my teacher. And I don't want to go to school!" Her voice rose in a wail.

"Come here, Amelia." Emily reached out a hand. "Tell me what you want to say and I'll write it for you. Then you can print your name at the bottom. You know how to do that."

With a loud sniff, Amelia went to Emily and wrapped her chubby arms around her neck. "I'm sorry, Em. It was all my fault. It was a stupid game."

"No, it wasn't," Emily said. "We just got carried away." She smiled. "I actually thought it was fun." And the very sort of game Miss Carr might've played when she was a little girl.

The day after the gold rush game, Emily was allowed to call on Mei Yuk as usual. Mei Yuk was delighted to hear that Emily had to work in her father's store, the way she, Mei Yuk, had to work in her father's restaurant.

At the end of their English lesson, Emily coaxed Sam away from his bone and left in good spirits. She loved Mei Yuk's latest drawing of Sam and couldn't wait to show it to Miss Carr. Maybe Miss Carr would invite Sam to her class. He could pose beside her dog, Watch. They'd be difficult to draw, but much more interesting than the stuffed raven that occupied the studio.

Maybe, once Miss Carr saw how talented Mei Yuk was, she'd invite her to join the class. If that were to happen, Emily wouldn't feel so bad about Mei Yuk's determination not to return to school.

But school was still three weeks away. Emily was thinking of all the things she wanted to do before the end of the holidays, when she saw Tom striding her way.

Her stomach twisted into a knot. She was halfway across the James Bay Bridge, so there were no shops to duck into, and it was too late to turn and gaze at the water, pretending she hadn't seen him. He'd already caught her eye. If he saw that she was avoiding him on purpose, he was sure to say something mean.

Sticks and stones may break my bones but names will never hurt me … She repeated the phrase for courage, but she knew it wasn't true. Words *could* hurt.

When they were face to face, Tom stopped and said, "Hello, Emily. I'm sorry about your bicycle."

Emily was speechless. An apology was the last thing she'd expected from Tom, especially one that sounded sincere. *Suspiciously* sincere.

"I only rode it the once," he said, "and I meant to give it back. But there've been a lot of things happening at home ..." He shrugged and smiled sheepishly. "Honest. I'm really sorry. But why aren't you riding it? There's nothing broken, is there?"

"No ... it's fine." She spoke cautiously, wondering if he were up to something. "I don't ride it to town because of Sam. He needs a leash with so many people around."

Tom crouched down and ruffled Sam's fur. "Hello, fella!"

Emily winced as Sam wagged his tail and licked Tom's hand, making happy nice-to-meet-you sounds. The traitor!

"Sure is a nice dog. Where did you get him?"

"I found him on the beach. The day you stole my bicycle."

"Borrowed." His eyes narrowed.

The knot in Emily's stomach grew tighter. *Stole* had been the wrong thing to say. If Tom were being sincere, she'd given him the perfect opening to change his tune. "I've got to get home," she said. "Come on, Sam."

"Wait a minute." Tom blocked her way. "You wouldn't want to sell Sam, would you? I need a dog."

"He's not for sale. And why do you need a dog?"

"You ought to know," he taunted. "Little Miss Murdoch, outfitter for the Klondike."

"You're going to the Klondike?" Emily felt such a surge of relief she wanted to whoop with joy. "When?"

"A week from Saturday. Pa and me, we're off on the *Bristol*. So do you see why I need the dog?"

"I suppose so, but you can't have mine." She elbowed her way past Tom and quickened her pace.

"Hey!" Tom caught up and grabbed her arm. "I really am sorry about your bicycle." His tone

71

turned nasty. "Sorry I didn't take it apart and sell it piece by piece. If it hadn't been for Alice snooping around—"

"Let go!" Emily yanked her arm, but the harder she tried to pull away, the tighter he squeezed. "You're hurting me!"

With a fierce growl, Sam lunged at Tom, forcing him to let go.

"Now leave me alone, you thief!" Emily hurled the words in Tom's face and stormed away.

"Call me a thief?" Tom yelled at her back. "What about you? I know who owns that dog! And he's going to want him back!"

For the rest of that day and into the night, Emily worried about Tom's parting words. He'd meant to upset her and he'd succeeded. But it couldn't be true. As Dr. Murphy had suggested, Sam's previous owner had probably thrown the dog overboard on purpose. He wouldn't want him back.

On the other hand, Tom may well have been speaking the truth.

"Oh, Sam," she whispered. He was the best dog in the world. She couldn't imagine losing him.

It was the last thought Emily had before falling asleep.

CHAPTER № 9

"... *six bottles of steak sauce, forty boxes* of candles, and eleven bars of soap. There, George. That's another one done." Emily added the items to a gold-seeker's outfit, checked them off a list, and moved on to the next outfit, leaving George to add the flour, salt, sugar, and lard. Other employees handled tools, equipment, clothing, and cases of canned food. Once the outfits were packed, they were set out on the street, ready to be picked up and hauled down to the docks. Then they were loaded onto a ship.

Emily was amazed at the number of boxes, kegs, and crates that made up one outfit. No wonder the ships rode low in the water, looking as though they might sink at any moment.

Her first afternoon at the store was going well. She and George worked side by side, bantering good-naturedly. Both agreed it was the most enjoyable punishment they'd ever had. But they wouldn't dare let on to their fathers.

At the end of their shift, Emily biked home. She had the rest of the afternoon planned. First, a ride around the neighbourhood with Sam. He loved to heel when she rode her bike, and he gave a little woof whenever she rang the bell. After that, she'd go to the park to feed the ducks and maybe call on Alice.

She turned the corner of her street, ringing the bicycle bell to let Sam know she was on her way. She began to feel uneasy when there was no response. And when she saw Amelia trudging across the lawn, Sam's leash in her hand, she knew that something was wrong.

She got off her bike, her heart in her throat. "Amelia …? What happened?"

Amelia's face was wet with tears. "I—I'm sorry," she stammered. "He looked so sad when you left. We only wanted to cheer him up, and he wasn't stubborn like before. He really *wanted* to go for a walk. So—so—" She started to cry.

By this time, Mother had joined them. She ushered them inside where a downcast Jane was waiting and, little by little, the story came out.

"We took Sam to the park," Amelia sniffed.

"I tried to hold on to the leash, but he was too strong," Jane said miserably. "He was chasing the ducks and he saw a squirrel and … and he ran off into the woods."

"We called and called. But he wouldn't come."

"We couldn't find him, but we found the leash." Jane risked a glance at Emily. "So someone …"

"Someone stole my dog!" Emily exploded. "How *could* you?" Her voice shook with tears and rage.

As her mother reached out to comfort her, Emily pushed her away and ran back outside. She got on her bike and pedalled furiously, calling for Sam, stopping only to ask passersby if they'd seen him.

When she got to the park, she asked everyone she met—children feeding the ducks, couples out for a stroll, a group of gold seekers training their dogs to wear a harness and pull a sled. Did they know anything? Did they look guilty?

Several people remembered seeing Sam chasing the ducks and squirrels, but no one knew where he had gone.

She searched the wild part of the park and the slopes of Beacon Hill, frantically calling his name. But there was no sign of him anywhere.

She left the park and biked along Dallas Road to the outer harbour. A gold seeker was the obvious culprit. He could be at the wharves right now, boarding a ship with Sam in tow.

Or it could have been that horrid Tom. She'd stop by his house, search it from top to bottom if she had to—but what if he'd sold Sam? Or what if he did know Sam's former owner? What if Tom had told him where to find Sam, and the brute had lurked around the Murdochs' house and followed Jane and Amelia to the park?

She took a deep breath and told herself to calm down. The hows and whys and what ifs didn't matter. All that mattered was finding her dog.

The last time she'd been at the wharves, she'd felt exhilarated by the highly charged atmosphere. With hundreds of people going off to seek their fortune, the sense of adventure was so strong she'd almost been able to taste it.

Now the scene was a nightmare. Two ships were in the harbour, one taking on cargo, the other taking it off. Throngs of people were milling about—passengers coming and going, getting off one ship or boarding the other, some with dogs, some without; friends and relatives greeting new arrivals or seeing off those who were departing.

She shuddered with despair. How could she hope to find Sam in such a mob?

"SAM!" She strained her voice, praying that it might be heard above the clamour: the hiss of steam winches loading and unloading cargo, the hammering of carpenters, the whinnying, bleating, and barking of horses, sheep, and dogs, the shouts, yells, and cries of people, and—to cap it off—the bawling of a herd of cattle about to be driven onto the northbound ship.

A tap on her shoulder made her jump. She turned, saw Alice, and wailed, "Sam's gone! I think Tom took him!" Between sobs, she told Alice what Tom had said the day before.

"Tom couldn't have taken him," Alice said, shaking her head. "He's been in the house all day, until now. We came to the wharf to meet my Uncle Ted. See that ship?" She pointed to the one that had just finished docking. "Uncle Ted's on it. He's going to the Klondike with Tom and Pa." Without warning, she threw her arms around Emily and burst into tears. "I'm sorry about Sam. But oh, Em! Ma's been in such a state ever since Pa decided he's going to the Klondike. He quit his job and there was a terrible row, and he's taking Tom to keep him out of trouble. I don't know what to do!"

"I'm sure things will be all right." Emily wasn't the least bit sure, but for a moment, she put aside her own worries and tried to reassure her friend. "They'll find some gold and be home in a twinkling. You'll hardly know they've been gone."

"I suppose you're right." Alice blew her nose and wiped her eyes. "You're the best friend I've ever had. You're always right. About Mei Yuk … and everything."

Emily felt a rush of emotion. With Tom out of the way, there was a good chance that she and Alice could renew their friendship. Mei Yuk might feel brave enough to go back to school. Alice's mother might even soften up a bit, with her husband far away. Life would be perfect. If only Sam were found.

CHAPTER N^o *10*

Black male dog, white chest and muzzle, tan markings on paws. Well behaved except with ducks and squirrels. Knows how to fetch, say please, and shake a paw. Loves sausages and bones. Answers to the name of Sam ...

Over the next two weeks, Emily and everyone she knew asked about Sam. Her father placed an ad in the newspaper. Murdoch and Walsh put a large notice in the store window. Nothing helped.

She kept waking up in the night, thinking she'd heard Sam's woof at the back door or the sound of his toenails clicking on the kitchen floor. She got up in the morning hoping to see him lolling on the verandah or snoozing under the breakfast table. Whenever she left the house, she prayed that she'd return to find him dozing under the maple tree, waiting for her.

It didn't help to hear that dogs of all shapes and sizes were selling like hotcakes—or that several neighbours had had a pet stolen from their own backyard. Or that Sam could already be on his way to the Klondike.

She went to the wharves at every opportunity, scanning the crowds, asking questions, calling his name. But time and again, she returned home empty-handed and disheartened.

Then came the day the *Bristol* was due to depart. It was an enormous ship and was said to be carrying the largest assortment of passengers and freight ever to set sail from a Pacific coast port—more than five hundred passengers and dogs, five hundred horses, mules, and oxen, and thousands of tons of cargo.

The wharf hummed with one of the largest crowds Emily had ever seen. Those people who hadn't come by foot had come by carriage, wagon, bicycle—even by canoe or rowboat, like George and Mr. Walsh, who had rowed up from the Gorge. Most had come to see the latest batch of gold seekers on their way, while others had shown up to gawk at the ship. Some, like her parents and sisters, were looking out for a black-and-white dog.

Emily managed to spot a few familiar faces. Mr. Sinclair was leaning over the ship's rail, waving his hat to catch his wife's attention. Alice and her mother were standing at the foot of the gangplank, giving farewell hugs to Tom, Mr. Kerr, and Uncle Ted.

Emily tried to take it all in. How much time was left before the ship set sail? The remaining outfits were being piled into nets, hoisted up from the wharf, and dropped into the ship's hold. The animals had already been herded aboard. But a seemingly endless line of passengers was still waiting on the dock and inching its way up the gangplank.

From her vantage point, she had a good view of the gangplank and paid close attention to the dogs that were accompanying the passengers. Many yapped excitedly, as high-spirited as their owners. Some looked cowed or confused. A few, dragged by ropes, were desperately trying to break free.

Suddenly, Emily's heartbeat quickened. A black dog, halfway up the gangplank, white muzzle, white chest—"Sam!" she bellowed.

Somehow, he heard her above the din. Ears cocked, he looked in her direction, straining against the rope that held him.

Emily burst through the crowd, desperate to save Sam before it was too late. The cargo would soon be loaded and the last passenger would be on board. The crew would haul up the gangplank and untie the moorings. The ship would leave the harbour and Sam would be gone forever.

"Hey! Stop, Miss!" At the foot of the gang-plank, the man taking tickets tried to stop her. "You can't go up there!"

"I'm getting my dog!" Without stopping to argue, she darted away from his outstretched arm and flew onto the gangplank.

The passengers were too busy waving goodbye to the crowd to notice. Ducking under their arms or skirting behind their backs, Emily reached the top of the gangplank and stepped onto the deck.

The crush of people, dogs, and cargo took her breath away. Passengers were standing ten deep at the railing, straining for a last sight of home or loved ones. Those who weren't at the railing swarmed about the deck or the stairways, anxious for the journey to begin.

"Sam!" She meant it as a shout. It came out a croak. He could be anywhere. In the hold, on one of the lower decks, in any number of cabins. It was hopeless.

She pushed through one group after another. Mostly men, a few ladies, even a couple of families with young children. She tugged on coats, interrupted conversations, and pleaded for help. "Have you seen a black dog ..."

They'd seen dozens of dogs! But one matching Sam's description? No.

As she was questioning the passengers, a ruckus broke out on the far side of the deck. Loud, angry voices were competing with the snaps and growls of unruly dogs.

One voice rose above the rest. "You can say what you like, but that's not your dog!"

Mr. Sinclair! Emily would have known his Scottish brogue anywhere.

"Well, I'm telling you it is!" another man was shouting. "I bought him fair and square."

"You never did!"

As other voices joined in, Emily struggled to get closer. "Sam!" she cried. "Here, Sam!"

The crowd stepped aside as she ran across the deck.

Hearing her voice, Sam gave a ferocious yank and broke free of the rope. He shot forward and

Sam shot forward and bounded into her arms, a squirming bundle of lapping tongue and walloping tail.

bounded into her arms, a squirming bundle of lapping tongue and walloping tail.

"There you go, Mister," someone said. "No better proof than that."

When Emily finally looked up, the man who'd either taken Sam or bought him from someone else had disappeared in the crowd. She didn't care. All that mattered—

At that moment, the steam whistle shrieked. The sound set the dogs howling. Any passenger who wasn't already at the rail stampeded over to get as close as they could.

The whistle shrieked again. Then a tremendous cheer erupted, echoed by all those on shore. "KLONDIKE, HO!"

Emily felt a rolling motion and sprang to her feet in alarm.

As she had feared, the gangplank had been raised. The lines had been cast, and the ship was leaving the dock.

CHAPTER *No" 11*

"It won't be long now," Mr. Sinclair said. He'd alerted the captain to Emily's predicament, the ship had slowed down, and the crew had rigged a cargo net to the winch. Emily and Sam had been lifted inside.

A crewman was going with them, lifebuoy in hand. He gave Emily an encouraging smile. "When we swing the net out over the water, try not to look down."

"You'll be fine, lass," said Mr. Sinclair. "Don't be afraid."

Afraid? Emily was terrified. A few moments

earlier, she'd been gaping at the widening space between the ship and the shore. Now she was inside a cargo net, huddling on a wooden pallet with one arm around Sam and the other holding onto the crewman.

"All set!" he cried.

Mr. Sinclair tipped his hat and grinned. "You're a Murdoch and Walsh special!"

Emily tried her best to return his smile.

"Don't worry," the crewman said kindly. "This net can carry two tons at a time."

Emily gritted her teeth. She felt the net sway as it was hoisted up and over the railing and then— oh! The windblown, heart-stopping swing as it was slowly lowered down to the sea.

In spite of the crewman's warning, Emily looked down. She was amazed to see George and Mr. Walsh rowing towards the ship. As the net came down, Mr. Walsh reached up and grabbed hold. He guided the net into the rowboat and loosened the top. Then he helped Emily and Sam out while George kept the rowboat steady.

Anxious to be on their way, the crew of the *Bristol* was already winching up the crewman. He waved at Emily and said, "That wasn't so bad, was it?"

Emily shook her head and smiled. Then she buried her face in Sam's fur, too overcome to speak.

CHAPTER N.º 12

On the Sunday before school started, Murdoch and Walsh organized an outing to Cadboro Bay, a popular spot on the east side of Victoria. Three horse-drawn hay wagons were hired for the occasion, with enough room for employees, families, and friends, as well as several bulging picnic hampers.

Mei Yuk and her brothers were given permission to attend the party and so was Alice. Emily didn't know if this marked a permanent change in Mrs. Kerr's attitude towards the Chinese, but it was a hopeful sign—especially since Mrs. Kerr hadn't made a fuss when Alice announced that Mei Yuk would be returning to school.

The hayride took them through acres of rolling fields and farmlands. Songs were sung in exuberant voices, with each wagonload of singers trying to outdo the others. Sam added to the merriment by barking greetings to every cow, horse, and dog they passed.

When they arrived at the bay, they spread rugs and tablecloths on the sandy beach and set out the picnic. Fried chicken, sausages, roast beef, ham, salad, tomatoes, pickles, preserves, bread rolls, biscuits, lemonade, raspberry cordial—there was enough to feed the navy.

After eating and drinking their fill—at least until tea time—the girls helped Mei Yuk build her first sandcastle. Later, they played hopscotch in the sand, hunted for beach treasures, and splashed in the sea. Later still, the whole party got together for an improvised game of baseball.

As the sun was setting, everyone helped gather wood for a fire. More food and drink came out of the hampers. Lemon tarts, plum cake, almond cake, apple crisp—and leftovers from the earlier meal if anyone was still hungry.

The sky grew dark. A hint of autumn chilled the air. After everyone had wrapped themselves up and found a place near the bonfire, Emily's father stood up, raised his glass of raspberry cordial, and said, "I propose a toast."

Emily groaned inwardly. *Toasts?* They were for Christmas and New Year's, not summer. Stand up, sit down, on and on …

Father seemed to know what she was thinking, for he winked at her and said, "Two toasts only. And no need to raise yourselves, only your glasses." He looked over at George's father. "Walsh, why don't you start?"

"Right!" he said, raising his glass. "To the success of Murdoch and Walsh! May the Klondike be worth its weight in gold."

"To Murdoch and Walsh!" the party chorused.

"And a toast to all of us," Father said. "Thank you for sharing this day."

"To all of us!" the chorus went, with applause and hearty good wishes.

"And that's another summer gone," said Father.

Emily threw her arms around Sam and hugged him. "We'll never have another summer like this one," she said. "Will we, Sam?"

"Woof!"

Everyone laughed.

"I've got a game," Amelia piped up. "You tell everybody your favourite thing that happened this summer. Then you say what you wish for *next* summer. George, you start."

Emily listened as the game passed from one person to another. Surrounded by family and friends, and with Sam at her side, she didn't care what might happen in the future. She couldn't wish for a better time than the present.

Dear Reader,

This has been the fourth and final book about Emily. We hope you've enjoyed meeting and getting to know her as much as we have enjoyed bringing her—and her wonderful story—to you.

Although Emily's tale is told, there are still eleven more terrific girls to read about, whose exciting adventures take place in Canada's past—girls just like you. So do keep on reading!

And please—don't forget to keep in touch! We love receiving your incredible letters telling us about your favourite stories and which girls you like best. And thank you for telling us about the stories you would like to read! There are so many remarkable stories in Canadian history. It seems that wherever we live, great stories live too, in our towns and cities, on our rivers and mountains. We hope that Our Canadian Girl *captures the richness of that past.*

Sincerely,
    Barbara Berson

1608
Samuel de Champlain establishes the first fortified trading post at Quebec.

1759
The British defeat the French in the Battle of the Plains of Abraham.

1812
The United States declares war against Canada.

1845
The expedition of Sir John Franklin to the Arctic ends when the ship is frozen in the pack ice; the fate of its crew remains a mystery.

1869
Louis Riel leads his Métis followers in the Red River Rebellion.

1871
British Columbia joins Canada.

1755
The British expel the entire French population of Acadia (today's Maritime provinces), sending them into exile.

1776
The 13 Colonies revolt against Britain, and the Loyalists flee to Canada.

1837
Calling for responsible government, the Patriotes, following Louis-Joseph Papineau, rebel in Lower Canada; William Lyon Mackenzie leads the uprising in Upper Canada.

1867
New Brunswick, Nova Scotia and the United Province of Canada come together in Confederation to form the Dominion of Canada.

1870
Manitoba joins Canada. The Northwest Territories become an official territory of Canada.

1762
Elizabeth

Timeline

1885
At Craigellachie, British Columbia, the last spike is driven to complete the building of the Canadian Pacific Railway.

1898
The Yukon Territory becomes an official territory of Canada.

1914
Britain declares war on Germany, and Canada, because of its ties to Britain, is at war too.

1918
As a result of the Wartime Elections Act, the women of Canada are given the right to vote in federal elections.

1945
World War II ends conclusively with the dropping of atomic bombs on Hiroshima and Nagasaki.

1873
Prince Edward Island joins Canada.

1896
Gold is discovered on Bonanza Creek, a tributary of the Klondike River.

1905
Alberta and Saskatchewan join Canada.

1917
In the Halifax harbour, two ships collide, causing an explosion that leaves more than 1,600 dead and 9,000 injured.

1939
Canada declares war on Germany seven days after war is declared by Britain and France.

1949
Newfoundland, under the leadership of Joey Smallwood, joins Canada.

1897
Emily

1885
Marie-Claire

1939
Ellen

Check out the
OUR CANADIAN GIRL website

FUN STUFF
- E-cards
- Contests
- Recipes
- Activities and crafts

FAN AREA
- Fan guest book
- Photo gallery
- Downloadable OUR CANADIAN GIRL tea party kit

Get to know the girls! What does Angelique dream about? What is most important to Millie? What does Izzie long for?

www.ourcanadiangirl.ca